NEW YORK RAVE FLYERS

1991 - 1995

For Ernie Villalobos

STORM
NEW LOCATION
SEPTEMBER 19, 1992
sr
HARDCORE
11PM – SUNRISE

It's hard to believe that there has yet to be a true rave scene in New York City. There are those who have never been to a real rave. Then there are those who claim to be ''Rave Promoters'' who do it for the green and not for the scene.

After intense research the Storm Rave Organization will be throwing the deepest, most hardcore rave EVER in New York City. It will be the most advanced rave and superior to any event ever put on in the tri-state area.

We want to prove that this movement can shape the future. Anyone who was at our June 20th event knows what we are talking about. We also apologize about the closing of our July 18th event. We should have known better to go into the corporate world of Manhattan!

Going Back to Basics . . .Brooklyn's in the House!!!

PEACE . .

STORM ⟨sr⟩ RAVE
IF IT'S NOT STORM, YOU AIN'T GETTING WET . . .
SEPTEMBER 19, 1992
YOUR DESTINY AWAITS

PLUS: THE RAVERS, CAFFEINE, EVOLUTION, NASA, MATTE SILVER, MENTAL UNITY TRIBE, N.J. UNDERGROUND, L.I. TOOTHPASTE POSSE, SCOTTO, DB, LIQUID SKY, B-91, MOBY, CATASTROPHIC D.C., A RAVE CALLED QUEST RI, DAVE TRANCE, DAVID MENA, PROGRAM 2, YELLOW MAGAZINE, PLANET X, AMOEBAHEAD & MELLO MELLO, LOOP D.C., BIG FUNHOUSE, FRED STRONG, NEIL RUSH, THIRD PLANET AND YOU.

99.9%
IDIOT FREE
NASACELL®
YOU CANT BEAT THE RAVE TOP!
X-TREME NRG
X-TREME NRG
PATENTED
NASA RAVE, INC.
DB + SCOTTD
PATENTED
NASA RAVE, INC.
DB + SCOTTD
NASACELL®
NASACELL®
POWER FOR '93
POWER FOE '93
THIS ONE REALLY KEEPS ON GOING + GOING + GOING + GOING + GOING + GOING

MISSION CONTROL: DB + SCOTTO

NASA ORBITING DJ'S
KEOKI + JASON JINX + ON-E + POWER HOUR BY MR. KLEEN

AUDIO VIBRATIONS
RAVE + TEXNO + BASTARD HARD HOUSE

LIQUID SKY ROOM DJ'S
DB + SCOTT RICHMAN

AUDIO VIBRATIONS II
AMBIENT + TRANCE

STIMULANTS
SMART BAR + DUMB BAR

PSYCHECYBERADIANT LIGHTS
SCOTTO + JOSH

VISUAL STIMULI
BRAD BAKERS X-FX

HUMAN ACCEPTANCE
ALL AGES

STAR DATE
FRIDAY 1.22.93 • 11PM UNTIL DAZEBREAK

OUTPUT
$10 WITH INVITE TIL MIDNITE • $12 AFTER

LAUNCH PAD: THE SHELTER
157 HUDSON ST. 3 BLKS BELOW CANAL

REJUVENATION
COMPLIMENTARY SUNRIZE BREAKFAST

RAVE LINE
NYC 212 330 8233 / OUTSIDE NYC 1-800-4-RAVE-LINE

DESIGN: DB FOR CREATION UK + REB FOR ARTS SAKE

LIVE

TASTI BOX

FEATURING

KEOKI

**

rave-e-on
nasa's lunar water
MISSION CONTROL • DB + SCOTTO
rave-e-on
nasa's lunar water
MISSION CONTROL • DB + SCOTTO
50.7fl. oz. (1qt. 1pt. 2.7 fl. oz.)
Friday, December 18, 1992

NASA
NOCTURNAL AUDIO + SENSORY AWAKENING
MISSION CONTROL • DB & SCOTTO
FRIDAY 21ST AUGUST • 11PM TO SUNRISE
TIME CAPSULE 1
FRANKIE BONES
DB
SOUL SLINGER
ON-E
JASON JINX
JACQUELYN CHRISTIE
LIQUID SKY ROOM
DANTE
MR KLEEN
SMART BAR, MARTINS DUMB BAR
LIQUID SKY PRODUCTS + TOYS
LIGHTS: PSYCHECYBERADIANT
LAUNCH PAD: THE SHELTER 157 HUDSON STREET
3 BLOCKS BELOW CANAL
$10 WITH INVITE TIL MIDNITE • $12 AFTER
RAVE LINE : 212 330 8233 • BAL/DC 301 783 5492
A PORTION OF ALL PROCEEDS GO TO SAVE OUR PLANET
DESIGN: CREATION UK

Caffeine

january 20th, 1995 • 10pm until ?
AN ALL NIGHT
grand re-opening celebration

PREMIERING OUR ALL-NEW SLAMMIN' 30,000 WATTS OF SOUND AND TEARING UP THE TURNTABLES:

roger "wild child" mc kenzie
(U.K.)

scott henry
(FEVER, BALTIMORE)

james christian
(LIMELIGHT, CAFFEINE)

terry mullen
(CHICAGO)

frankie bones
(GROOVE WORLD, BROOKLYN)

onionz
(EDDY RECORDS, CAFFEINE)

dna
(MOTION, CAFFEINE)

micro
(CAFFEINE, SORTED RECORDS)

adam x

dave trance
(CAFFEINE RECORDS)

jo-jo
(DIGITAL CONFUSION)

Keep the RAW VIBE in WAREHOUSE C • 100% legal, safe & Underground
with a special live performance by "RHYTHM METHOD"
admission $12, $10 with invite • complimentary breakfast
plus ... special djs adding spice and keeping it nice!

MAIN INFO LINES:
516.951.1170 (motion/generic)
516.547.6137
516.242.1773

TOAST: 516.345.5517
ROBYN: 516.254.3651
ENERGIZER RABBIT: 718.390.8930
CURIOUS: 516.344.7157
FRANK: 212.435.3128

STOFER: 516.389.0392
JOINT VENTURES: 212.429.2041
DAVID: 314.994.1114 (St. Louis)
KEDRICK: 215.334.2342 (Philly)
DEREK/TRANSFUSED: 804.748.2000 (Va)

PROMO/THANKS: Harv-e, Jeff H, Slip Shod Rob, Kort & Greg, TWR, Tim, Mason, Puke, Tanya, Jon & Phil, R.J., Raeann, John
ADVANCE TICKETS at BUGG 797-7196/BACKDOOR RECORDS 797-7192

836 Grand Blvd, Deer Park, NY 11729 • (516) 242-1773 • (516) 547-6137

LIE EAST: Exit 52 make right onto Commack Rd. Go 2 1/2 miles to Grand Blvd. (corner 7/11). Make left at light. Club is 1/2 mile on right.
LIE WEST Exit 53. Follow Service Road to Commack Rd. (County Road 4). Make left. Go 2 1/2 miles to Grand Blvd. (corner 7/11). Make left at light. Club is 1/2 mile on right.
SO. STATE. Exit 39 north. Go 1/2 mile. Fork right onto Commack Rd. Go 1 mile to Grand Blvd. (corner 7/11). Make right at light. Club is 1/2 mile on right.

1993
NASALAND
Sound System
NASA
Ages 16+up
United States
USA
NASA

Creativity and Quality Craftmanship are the key ingredients in this and all NASA brand dancing sets. The specialized DJs in this NASA set are specially designed to add to the fun and excitement of dancing and playing with action-packed models that look like the real thing. Like all NASA DJ sets, this set provides endless dancing possibilities, and offers children the opportunity to achieve a feeling of pride and accomplishment while developing creativity. And it's fun! New and different fun every week. NASA events are carefully crafted from high quality plastics. They snap together firmly, yet mellow out easily, even after years of hard play. And remember - DJs from all NASA sets are designed to work together - so the DJs from this set can be combined with DJs from future NASA sets for added play value and fun!

35

- Scotto + DB.

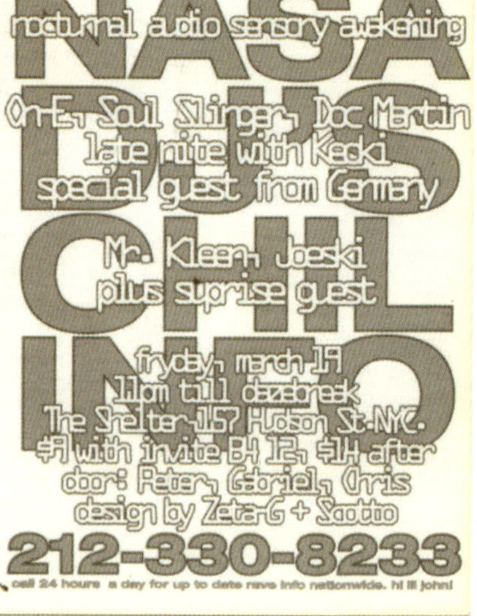

RAVEOLYMPIA PRESENTS
immortality
1999
sunday july 4th
independance day weekend
THE Caffeine TOUR

area 001

micro new york, caffeine records
without a doubt one of the most sought after artist in the united states. Dj
micro continues to rock crowds everywhere. more importantly, however, is the fact
that he is respected as a true pioneer of the east coast dance movement, regarded
as a 'techno maestro' micro will captivate your mind as your body moves to a
hard hitting beat. do not miss this legendary performer.

frankie bones new york sonic groove, caffeine records
the one and only. the man that needs no introduction. prepare yourselves for legendary,
slamming set of techno by one of the only artist in the world that can deliver.

x dream new york, caffeine records
the man behind caffeine the club, and now the label in a rare LA performance.
the backbone of the tour, we are extremely excited to have him join us as
part of this top notch line-up of this long awaited tour.

john debo boston, caffeine records
a masterful set of progressive trance by the east coast talent.

onion2 chocolate factory, new york, caffeine records

area 002

mark lewis immortality 98, phat phlunk records

dj messiah raver immortality 98.

dj d:fuse

jason blakemore

jamie thinnes

merlyn

PRE-SALE TICKET OUTLETS
20 PRE-SALE 25 AT THE EVENT
DOORS OPEN AT 9 PM TILL SUNLIGHT
new event venue limited capacity
this event will be 16 over bring ID
(this event will sell out get your
pre-sale ticket early.
tons of free CAFFEINE giveaways
tons of free PHATT PHLUNK giveaways

LOS ANGELES/MELROSE
Booth 7 clothing
7578 melrose ave. Hollywood
323.651.1373

Dmc records
7619 melrose ave. Hollywood
323.651.3520

SILVERLAKE/HOLLYWOOD
(rotterdam)

SAN FERNANDO VALLEY

SANTA MONICA/VENICE

SAN BERNARDINO/RIVERSIDE

EVENT & LOCATION INFO

sr

Caffeine
Presents
SONIC

SONIC II

JULY 28th 1995

DJ's

JOHN DEBO
MINDWARP REC

CHRIS FORTIER
ORLANDO

Micro
SORTED REC

DAVE TRANCE
PSYCHOACTIVE REC

DNA
BACKDOOR REC

Visual Outdoor Chillout / Japanese Animation

Come celebrate
THAT'S KRAFTY
Birthday with
Free Buffet

Free Whistle Giveaways
18 over $8 w/pass
21 over $6 w/pass

Doors Open 11pm
Advance tix @ Bugg (516) 797-7196 Info Lines: (516) 951-1170 • (516) 242-1773
Coming soon Warehouse B

ABSOLUT
Nocturnal Audio Sensory Awakening
NASA
Do not try to interpret
or explain the word Rave
to someone who has not experienced the
pure ecstasy of being in total harmony with
his or her surroundings, i.e. the feeling of
safety dancing within a crowd of
smiling faces, or the rush of a D J
taking you on a mind trip down into deep
dark caverns of trance and then up to the
highest peaks of spiritual Utopia.......
Do not try to explain.
Just tell them to open their minds.
100% PURE
MISSION CONTROL : DB + SCOTTO
HOMEGROWN
ABSOLUT RAVE.

JOIN THE NEXT GENERATION

NASA

MISSION CONTROL: SCOTTO + DB
FRIDAY 28TH AUGUST : 11PM TO DAZE BREAK

TIME CAPSULE 1
DB
JASON JINX
ON-E
DANTE
GUEST
JAMES CHRISTIAN
LIQUID SKY ROOM
SOUL SLINGER
MR KLEEN
SMART BAR + MARTIN'S DUM BAR
LIQUID SKY PRODUCTS + TOYS

PSYCHECYBERADIANT LIGHTS : SCOTTO

LAUNCH PAD : THE SHELTER 157 HUDSON STREET
3 BLOCKS BELOW CANAL
$10 WITH INVITE TIL MIDNIGHT : $12 AFTER
RAVE LINE : 212 330 8233 : BAL/DC 301 783 5492
A PORTION OF ALL PROCEEDS GO TO SAVE OUR PLANET

DESIGN : CREATION UK + IQ

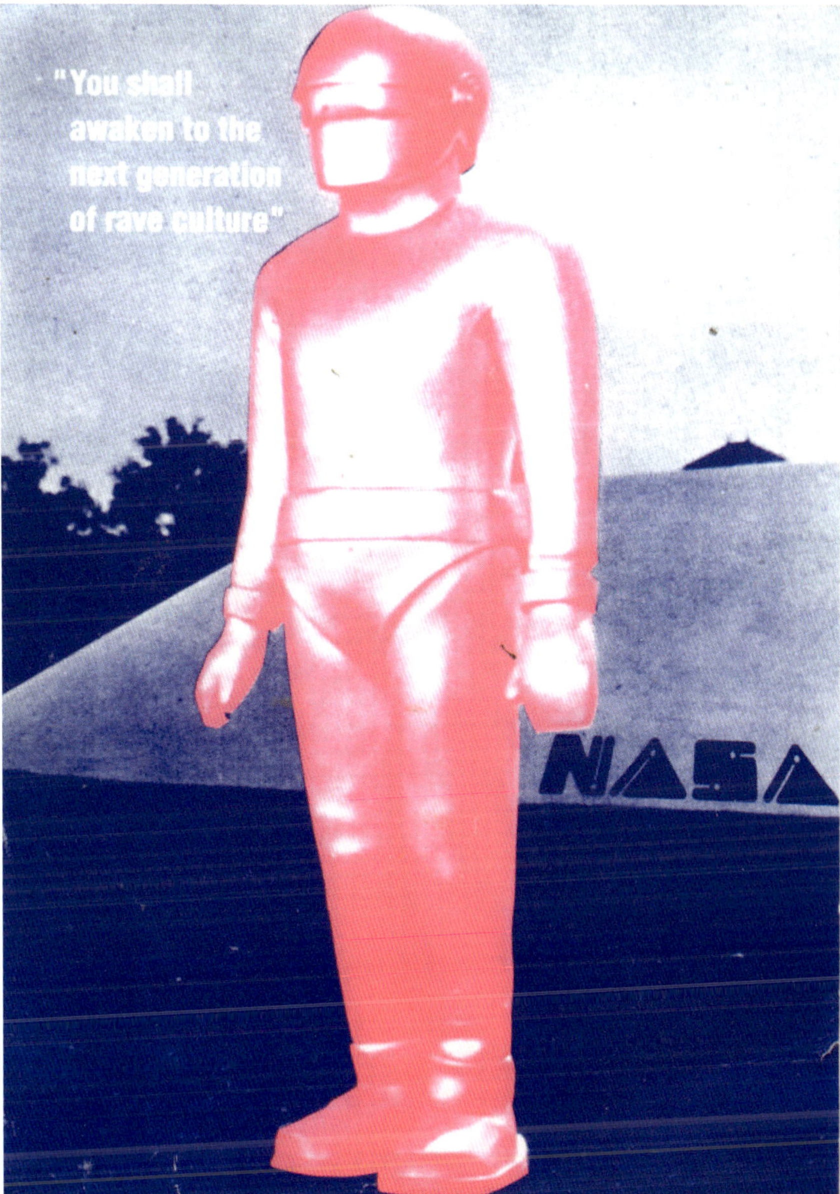
"You shall awaken to the next generation of rave culture"
NASA

N!ASA

NOCTURNAL AUDIO + SENSORY AWAKENING

MISSION CONTROL ★ SCOTTO, DANTE & DB

TIMECAPSULE ONE

ASTRO DJ'S GO INTO ORBIT ON THE MOST TECHNOLOGICALLY ADVANCED
SOUND SYSTEM IN THE GALAXY

DB • SOUL SLINGER • JASON JINX • ON-E
SPECIAL GUEST APPEARANCE • MOBY

TIMECAPSULE TWO

AMBIENT TRANCE DJ'S

DANTE • MR KLEEN • JACQUELYN CHRISTIE

VISUAL STIMULATION SCOTTO & CREATION UK

LIFT OFF: FRIDAY 7.24.92

FLIGHT DURATION: 11ᴾᴹ UNTIL SUNRISE

[THEN TRAVEL 3 BLOCKS TO ANOTHER DIMENSION OUTDOORS • SUNRISE UNTIL NOON]

NO M.C.S • NO CLUB POLITICS • NO GUEST LIST • NO VIP ROOMS • NO OVERBLOWN EGOS

SMART BAR & DUMB BAR • ALL AGES

LAUNCH PAD "THE SHELTER" 157 HUDSON ST., JUST BELOW CANAL

$12 WITH THIS FLYER

INFO: 212 330 8233

WARNING YOU MAY BURN UP ON RE-ENTRY

A PORTION OF ALL PROCEEDS GO TO SAVE THE PLANET

NASA Celebrates 50 Years of Mind Exploration

Scotto & DB present a celebration of 30 years of
mind exploration
friday 4.16.93
"our music is the drug..."
suprise LIVE performance
by one of NASA's faves

experience an unparallelled 16 head
LASER SHOW
driven by Scotto

Mind Expanding DJ's:
Dmitry (Deee-Lite)
Destructo (Rave America)
Jason Jinx (Nasa)
Troposphere (Nasa)
DB (Losing his Mind)

NYC's only ambient dance floor
presents Muzak by Minus-8
featuring John Hall and Adam Goldstone
with visuals by Eno-One

11pm until Dazebreak
$9 with flyer before 12, $14 after.
Shelter. 157 Hudson St. 3 Blocks below Canal.
24 hour rave info: 212.330.8233.

HEY! Get involved in recycling!!!
It's Earth Day 1993-
Do YOU know where your trash is?
As always, a portion of all proceeds
go to Greenpeace.

graphics: DB for Creation UK + Zeta-G

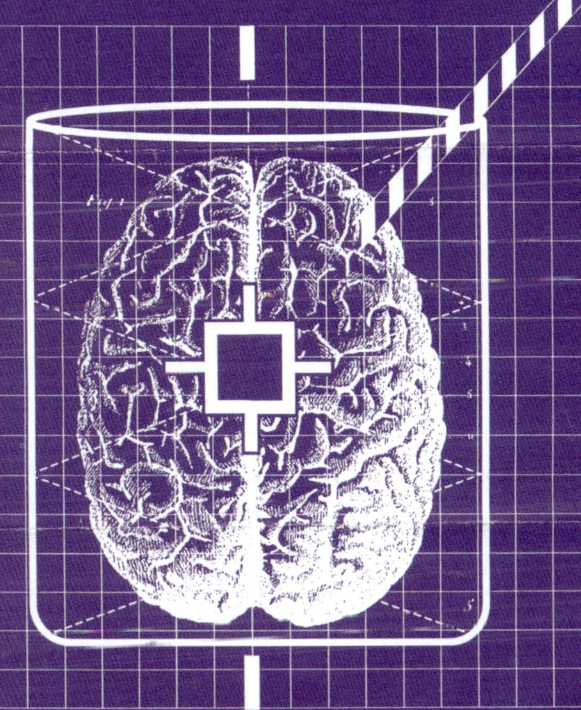

brain sr Storm
June 20, 1992
12 MIDNIGHT TILL 9 AM . . . 100% HARDCORE

In 1989, Frankie Bones became the only American DJ to become part of the London Orbital Rave Scene. In 1990 Storm was a vision, in 1991 that vision became reality. In 1992, with the help of the Storm organization and the 2500 people at our last rave, Storm became a legacy . . . Come and Join the Future.

Organization:
DAVE LIGHTS
MR. HYDE
JOEY FAX
FRANKIE BONES

TICKETS $15.00
FREE WITH NMS BADGE

STORM RAVE
PRESENTS

Promo Team
HEATHER HEATHER
NEIL RUSH
FRED STRONG
GROOVE RECORDS
JENNA & DEB

BRAIN STORM

NEW YORK'S OFFICIAL HARDCORE RAVE HAPPENS JUNE 20, 1992
LIVE PERFORMANCES BY:

PWL INTERNATIONAL, LONDON
TOXIC TWO
"RAVE GENERATOR"
RAY LOVE & DAMON WILDS
TOP 10 LONDON HIT,
PLUS NEW TRACKS

QUARK RECORDS
EUPHORIA
AMERICA'S RAVE SENSATION
PERFORMING CUTS OFF THE
EUPHORIA E.P.

BROOKLYN GROOVE PRODUCTIONS
FRANKIE BONES
FEATURING: **MARCELINA**
"RUSH TO THE RHYTHM"
WORLD PREMIER OF BROOKLYN'S NEW
TECHNO ANTHEM

— HOSTED BY DENNIS THE MENACE —

WORLD CLASS DJ LINE UP

NEW YORK
ADAM X
NEW YORK'S HARDCORE GENERAL
LENNY DEE
FROM INDUSTRIAL STRENGTH RECORDS
JIMMY CRASH
FROM DIRECT DRIVE RECORDS
RALPHIE DEE
FROM THE GROUP "NORTHERN LIGHTS,"
NEXT PLATEAU RECORDS
REPETE
OF FUTURE SHOCK, LIMELIGHT
ANTHONY ACID
OF VORTEX RECORDS PREMIERING "THE EPIC"

GERMANY
SVEN VÄTH
FROM HARTHOUSE RECORDS

**PLUS OTHERS
TO BE CONFIRMED**

THIS EVENT
WILL BE VIDEOTAPED
FOR T.V.

LOS ANGELES
DOC MARTIN
THE WEST COAST'S #1 RAVE DJ
MATT C.
FROM THE FAMOUS "FLAMMABLE LIQUID"
CHRIS CRUNCH
OF R.E.A.L.

DETROIT
RITCHIE HAWTIN
OF PLUS 8 RECORDS PRODUCER OF CYBERSONIK

LONDON
CASPER POUND
OF THE RISING HIGH COLLECTIVE

MC AND SHOW HOST : **FRANKIE BONES**

TICKETS AVAILABLE FROM GROOVE RECORDS, 64 AVE U, BROOKLYN, NY FROM 8PM–2AM ON JUNE 20, OR THE STORM RAVE VAN AT THE MARRIOT BROADWAY, BET. 44 & 45 ST. FROM 10PM–5AM. THERE WILL BE OTHER PAYPOINTS AND TRANSPORATION CALL (718) 714-5232 OR BEEP (718) 766-5369. 40 K SOUND, INTELLABEAMS, DRINKS, TOYS, LASERS, BACKDROPS, PLUS THE USUAL STORM GOODIES . . .

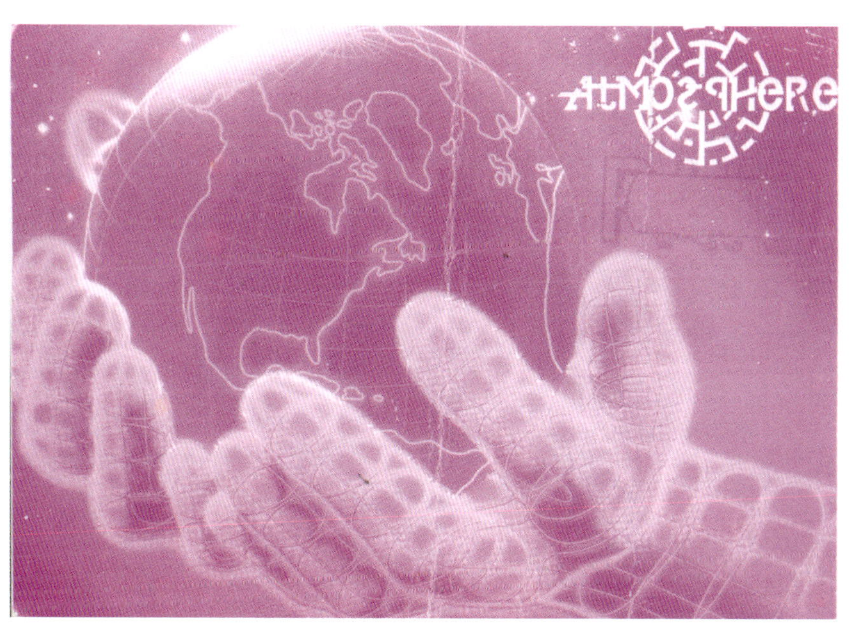

ATMOSPHERE

STOP THE VIOLENCE — FRANKIE BONES WAS ATTACKED LAST WEEK BY 4 YOUTHS WITH BATS IN FRONT OF HIS HOUSE. LEFT A BLOODY MESS. IT TOOK OVER FIFTY STITCHES TO CLOSE 5 WOUNDS TO THE HEAD. THIS HAPPENED BECAUSE ANOTHER PERSON WAS BEATEN UP BY AN UNKNOWN GROUP OF KIDS AT THE "FIELD OF DREAMS." OUR SOUND ENGINEER WAS ALSO HOSPITALIZED AFTER TRYING TO GATHER INFORMATION ABOUT THIS INCIDENT. WE AT ATMOSPHERE ARE PROMOTING **PEACE.** WE ARE NOT HOLDING ANY ORGANIZERS OF "FIELD OF DREAMS" RESPONSIBLE, BUT WE SUGGEST YOU LEAVE THE VIOLENCE HOME BECAUSE WE DON'T WANT ANYONE ELSE HURT.

★ ONE HOUSE UNDER ONE GROOVE, PEACE ★

BROOKLYN GROOVE PRODUCTIONS

PRESENT

SATURDAY, SEPT. 14, 1991

HARDCORE TECHNO BY GUEST DJ'S
DJ GONZO (B.G.P. Records)
TOMMY DUGO (B-91 WKRB)
JERRY JAM (Staten Island)

SATURDAY, SEPT. 21, 1991

EURO-TECHNO BY GUEST DJ's
DJ D.A.D. (Pirate Club, London)
MERU (Fabulous Foundation, London)
JASON JINX (Various, Long Island)

FRANKIE BONES
WORLD PEACE TOUR 1991

NEW YORK • PARIS • LONDON • ROME • LOS ANGELES • MANCHESTER
BERLIN • COPENHAGEN • GLASCOW • SAN FRANCISCO • TORONTO

IN-HOUSE DJ'S **ADAM X** & **JIMMY CRASH** • **LEE BOTIX** • **JEFF KAOS**
HOSTED & PRESENTED BY **TINA TRIPP** (718) 481-2905

DOORS OPEN: 10:00 P.M.
18 TO RAVE • 21 TO DRINK
ADMISSION: $12.00
LADIES FREE TILL MIDNIGHT
PROPER I.D., NO DRUGS

CLUB ATMOSPHERE (at Tropics)
22 WAVE STREET • STATEN ISLAND
VERRAZANO BRIDGE TO BAY STREET
LEFT AT LIGHT, 9 LIGHTS DOWN
BAY STREET TO WAVE STREET
HOTLINE (718) 816-0713

FILL OUT FOR $5.00 OFF AND MEMBERSHIP FOR FUTURE EVENTS

NAME ____

ADDRESS _________________________________ CITY, STATE, ZIP ____________

STAR TRIP
DEEP RAVE NINE
THE NASA GENERATION
"ENTERING THE WORM HOLE" STAR DATE: 1.29.93

NASA
NOCTURNAL AUDIO + SENSORY AWAKENING
MISSION CONTROL: DB + SCOTTO
NASA ORBITING DJ'S
DB + SOUL SLINGER + JASON JINX + ON-E
POWER HOUR BY JOEY BELTRAM
AUDIO VIBRATIONS
RAVE + TEXNO + BASTARD HARD HOUSE
LIQUID SKY ROOM DJ'S
MR KLEEN + TROPOSPHERE
AUDIO VIBRATIONS II
AMBIENT + TRANCE
STIMULANTS
SMART BAR + DUMB BAR
PSYCHECYBERADIANT LIGHTS
SCOTTO + ROY BOY
HUMAN ACCEPTANCE
ALL AGES
STAR DATE
FRIDAY 1.29.93 • 11PM UNTIL DAZEBREAK
OUTPUT
$10 WITH INVITE TIL MIDNITE • $12 AFTER
LAUNCH PAD: THE SHELTER
157 HUDSON ST. 3 BLKS BELOW CANAL
REJUVENATION
COMPLIMENTARY SUNRIZE BREAKFAST
RAVE LINE
NYC 212 330 8233 / OUTSIDE NYC 1-800-4-RAVE-LINE
DESIGN: DB FOR CREATION UK + REB FOR THE WHYOS

RAVE NEW WORLD
performing live
MOBY + PRODIGY
THE
with
CYBERSONIK
USA
UK
SOUND SYSTEM DJs
+8 RECORDS
RICHIE HAWTIN + J. ACQUAVIVA
SPECIAL GUEST DJ APPEARANCE BY MOBY
PSYCHECYBERADIANT LIGHTS BY SCOTTO
SATURDAY FEB 13   10:30pm
234 W 43 St.   THE ACADEMY
THANKS TO NASA + SATELLITE

RAVE NEW WORLD
PERFORMING LIVE
MOBY + THE PRODIGY
CYBERSONIK

Plus music non-stop
Djs Richie Hawtin and
John Aquaviva from +8
NASA Djs DB + Mr. Kleen
Guest Djs Moby and
Liam of The Prodigy
Lights by Scotto
Visuals by Brad Baker's X-FX
Smart Bar + Free Giveaways !!!

100% legal space
free whistles
All Ages
and lots of love.

Tickets $17.50, available at
Bleeker Bob's & at The Academy
the night of rave (234 W 43rd St.)
Saturday, February 13 10:30PM Sharp
Outside NYC: 1-800-4-RAVE-LINE
In NYC: NASA 212-330-8233
SATELLITE PRODS.: 212-465-3299

design: Zeta-G

SCOTTO
U4Eah!
100% GRAN

DON'T SMOKE, RAVE!
DB • SCOTTO
Mindfuck
COME TO NASA COUNTRY

FRIDAY 16 NOVEMBER 1992

NASA DJ'S
DB * ON-E * DANTE * MR KLEEN

PLUS SPECIAL GUESTS
SUPER DJ DMITRY
+
JUNGLE DJ TOWATO WA

PSYCHECYBERADIANT LIGHTS: SCOTTO

ALL AGES

LOCATION:
THE SHELTER, 157 HUDSON ST • 3 BLKS BELOW CANAL
$10 W/FLYER BEFORE MIDNIGHT $12 AFTER
RAVELINE'S: 212 330 8233 / BAL + DC: 301 783 5492
1 800 4 RAVE LIST

DESIGN: CREATION UK + REB

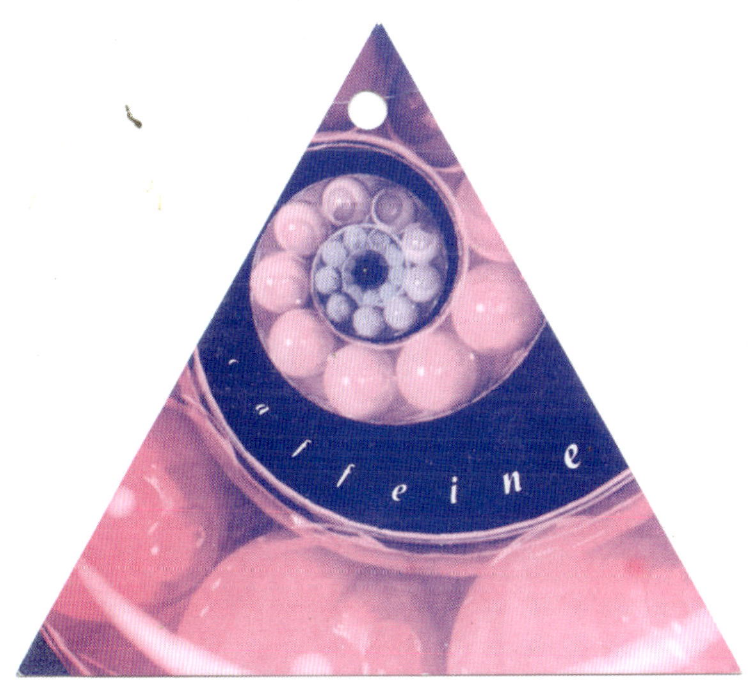
caffeine

fRidAY
mAY 21st
Caffeine
P R E S E N T S
micro · onionz · Dave Trance
AND SPECIAL GUEST DJ sameer
$2 off with pass
836 grand blvd. dix hills ny 11729 hotline 516.547.6137
lie exit 52 (commack rd) to grand blvd (corner 7-11) make left 1/2 mile on right
southern state exit 39 north (rte 231) to commack rd 1 mile make right onto grand blvd (corner 7-11) 1/2 mile on right

L.A. DAVE and TREPP
In Association with GROOVE RECORDS
Present a New Concept

DELIVERANCE

FRIDAY JULY 3, 1992   PART ONE

FRANKIE BONES

ON THIS NIGHT YOU WILL UNDERSTAND THE FUTURE OF UNDERGROUND MUSIC. WITH
ALL THE TECHNO "NOISE" GOING ON IN NEW YORK, FRANKIE WILL BE PLAYING
"TRIBAL HOUSE," A FRESH OUTLOOK ON YOUR DESTINY.
YOUR HOST — DENNIS THE MENACE

"THIS IS THE NEXT STEP TO THE WORD HARDCORE"
Special Thanks to STORM & CAFFEINE....

LOCATION: The WAREHOUSE right next to CAFFEINE/VOODOO 832-6 Grand Blvd.
Dix Hills, Long Island, NY Call (718) 714-5232 or (516) 242-1773

DOORS OPEN
10PM

THIS IS A ONE-OFF EVENT. BE THERE

LIE: Exit 52 South (Commack Rd.) to Grand Blvd. (corner 7-11) make left, 1/2 mile on right.
SOUTHER STATE: Exit 39 North (Rt. 231) to Commack Rd. 1 Mile make right onto
Grand Blvd. (corner 7-11) 1/2 mile on right.

$5 ADM
W/INVITE
$7 W/O

100% TRIBAL • JULY 3, 1992

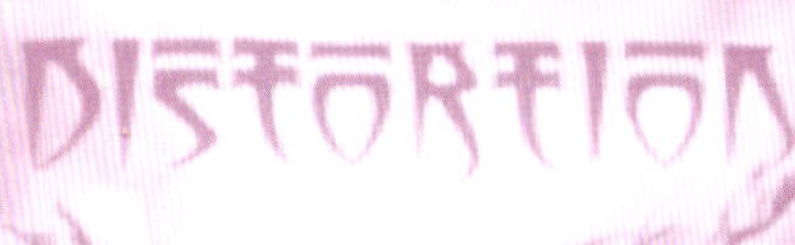
DISTORTION

THURSDAY
JULY 30, 1992

DOORS OPEN
10:00 PM

HARDCORE · TECHNO

BRANDON (VW) MARTIN P
BARRY B and J&J PRODUCTION

present the best in
TECHNO MUSIC from
EUROPE
starting
THURSDAY
JULY 30, 1992
at 10 p.m.

guest d.j.'s on the night
FRANKIE BONES
ADAM X + JIMMY CRASH
from **STORMrave + CAFFEINE**

visuals by **DAVE LIGHTS**
hosted by **WHITE GIRLS WITH SOUL**
promos by **DENNIS THE MENACE**

special thanks to
JOHNNY FALLACE

free deer park water

come in peace
admission $10

bonesdesign '92

DISTORTION
1414 Sheepshead Bay Road
Brooklyn, NY 11235
for info on the night, call
GROOVE (718) 714-5232

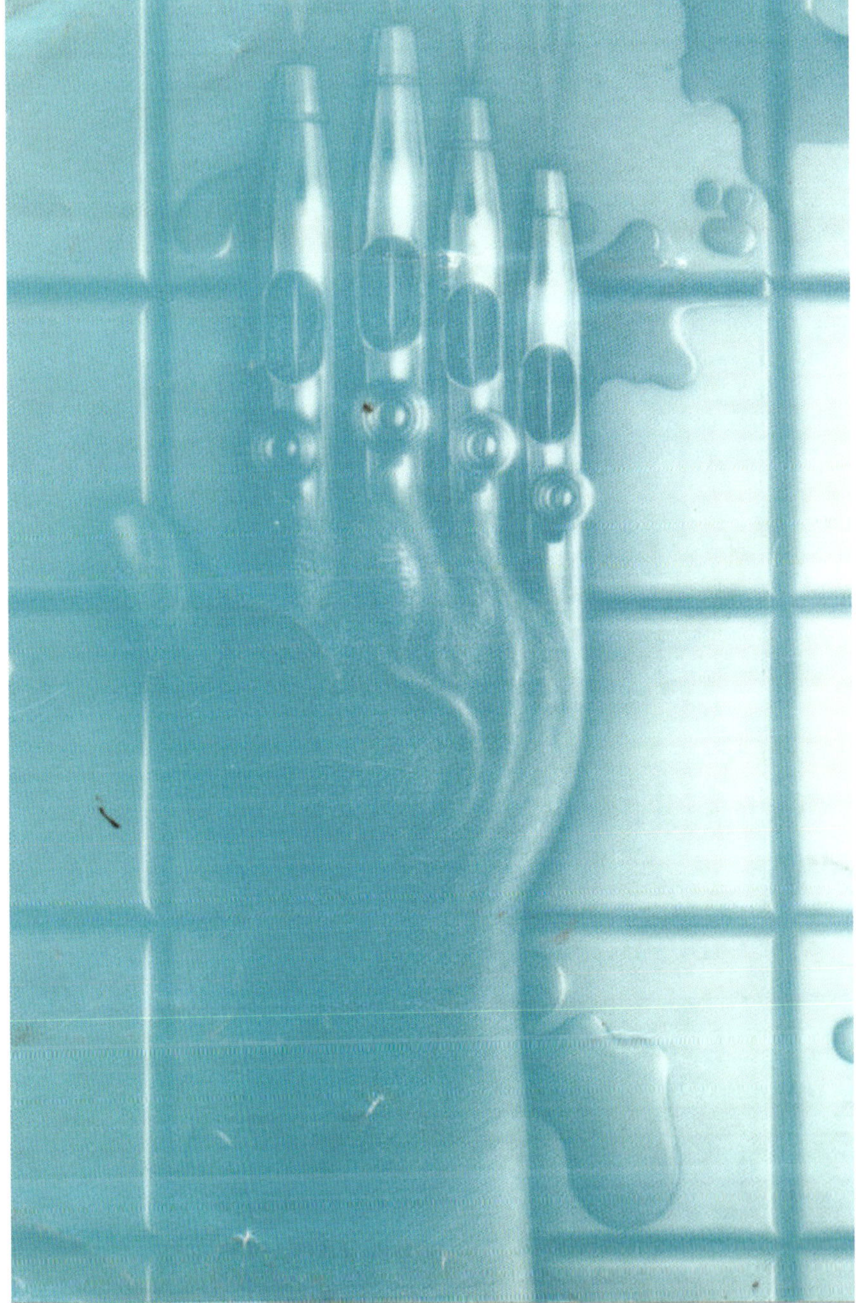

"A NIGHT OF OLD SCHOOL WAREHOUSE FUN!!"

FLASHBACK

GOING BACK TO THE EARLY DAZE OF RAVE

SATURDAY, SEPT. 26, 1992

DJ'S

FRANKIE BONES
OF STORM

DANTE
EVOLUTION

JAMES CHRISTIAN
STORM, FLUID

DAVE TRANCE
LIMELIGHT, CAFFIENE

MICRO
CAFFIENE

ONIONS
L.I. & BOSTON UNDERGROUND

AND LIVE FROM LONDON: **TIM TAYLOR**
PLAYING HIS MASSIVE HIT "THE HORN TRACK"

● FREE TOYS AND 20K OF POUNDING NOISE ●

HOTLINES CALL (212) 631-1065 / (212) 629-2061
TICKETS: GROOVE RECORDS (718) 714-5232
ON THE NIGHT: 9-26-92 FROM 8PM–1AM

★ FROM THE UNDERGROUND TO YOU ★

sr

A SCOTTO & DB Outer Space Publication.

At the Door, Peter, Gabriel & Chris.

Psychecyberadiant lights by Scotto and Josh.

NASA is located at the Shelter, 157 Hudson St. 3 blocks below Canal. Ages 16+ up.

FRIDAY, MAY 14, 1993

NEWSLINE

ENERGY ZONE 1:

DJ KEOKI:
Disco 2000, spinning ultratrance and mindwarp rhythms.

DJ DMITRY:
Deee-Lite, spinning a sampladelic mix of audio lightbeams.

DJ JASON JINX:
NASA, spinning the purest UK jungle and breakbeat.

DJ SEAN CIC:
Anarchic Adjustment, spinning hard German and Detroit techno.

DJ STEVE AUSTIN:
NASA Apollo Missions, spinning his favorite TV themes from the 70's.

LIVE PERFORMANCE: RHYTHM METHOD
performing their own brand of tribal techno.

CHILL ZONE 2:

DJ DB:
Studio 54, spinning a wild mix of new London disco and progressive house.

DJ TROPOSPHERE:
NASA, spinning his own brand of tribal and progressive.

CELEBRITY DJ STEVE AUSTIN comes out of exile this week to make an unexpected appearence at NASA. When asked why he wanted to spin after all this time, he replied "It was the Six Million Dollar fee they offered, and the fact that they had the technology."

NEGATIVE ENERGY FLASh: In a rare outburst, a raver had to be physically ejected from NASA last week after being told numerous times that none of the DJs would play Sesame's Treat. NASA's efficient security, photo above, quickly dealt with the young man and told him to **CENSORED** or **CENSORED**

NASA:Socially Aware Again.

Friday, the 14th sees the nation's launch of 'Rave for Choice'. They will be at NASA distributing literature and answering any questions about the organization. %10 of this week's proceeds will go to Rave for Choice.

Style Meets Technology:

Fashion Gurus Gabriel & Peter will be assisting Walter S. and Ernie Glam in producing a fashion show in the chillout room at NASA on Friday the 14th. The show is to spotlight the latest in dope ravegear. Designers featured will be Drop, Liquid Sky, Anarchic Adjustment, Aquasonic Funwear, Ding Dong School, 555 Soul, Cake, plus others to be announced. For information on the Style Summit, call 212-255-5499.

CRIME OF PASSION: In a bizzare legal story, a NYC graphics company, Creation UK, Inc., had their design wizz, DB, taken away by police officers yesterday in Manhattan. After ignoring several legal threats from Levy, Levy, and Bastard, on behalf of the Visa and Mastercard corporations for copyright infringements. Several officers handcuffed DB and took him into custody. Ironically, just as they were leaving, several other lawyers and police representing Evian, Duracell, Marlboro, Absolut Vodka, Wrigley's Gum, Bazooka, Alka Seltzer and Nike arrived to serve similar lawsuits. DB was last seen screaming from the back of the police car, "I did it for the Ravers!!!". Federal agents are currently searching for Zeta-G to take him into custody for questioning, but in a secret phonecall to NASA, he promised that he would still turn out flyers for the kids.

SUPER-BOWL
BLAST
THE SUPER BOWL OF MENTAL DJS
DON'T MISS THE LARGEST OUTDOOR JAM
X-TRAVAGANZA EVER IN N.Y.C!
6 OF NEW YORK CITYS HARDEST DJS
TO BLOW YOUR MIND ON 40,000
MEGAWATTS OF STUPID
HYPE SOUND
Early Palaeozoic
Middle Palaeozoic
Late Palaeozoic

MATT E SILVER • JACE RYAN • MAREK D-MADNESE
PRESENT
HARDHOUSE 10PM TILL 2AM
RAVE 2AM TILL...
BLAST
A FUEL EVENING OF HIGH INTENSITY FUN AND SOUND
HOST JAMIE TECH , ALCID, DAVID CAMERON, SEAN NUTLEY AND STACEY FINE
● WHERE
PIER 84 44TH S.T. WEST-SIDE HIGHWAY
● WHEN
WEDNESDAY JULY 17TH
RAINDATE
TUESDAY JULY 23RD
● TIME
2AM TILL... DAWN!!!
● DJ TODD TERRY
(KING OF THE DANCE FLOOR)
● DJ CHARLEY CASANOVA
(AMBASSADOR OF TECHNO)
● DJ LITTLE LOUIE VEGA
WITH KENNY DOPE
(1200 SUPERSTAR/MASTERS AT WORK)
● DJ LENNY DEE
(THE TECHNO HOODLUM)
● DJ JOEY BELTRAM
(ENERGY FLASH PURE XTASY)
● DJ KEOKI
(TECHNO TRIP KING)
● DJ REPEAT
(THE TECHNO KID)
● DJ MONEY PENNY
(TECHNO LOVE GODDESS)
● TRANSPORTATION
TAKE N, R TO TIMES SQUARE
WALK WEST TO WATER/TAKE CAB CAR
TO 44TH ST AND WEST SIDE HIGHWAY
PARKING AVAILABLE
IN ASSOCIATION WITH LIMELIGHT
STEVE LEWIS AND MICHAEL ALIG
● PLUS
SURPRISE GUESTS PERFORMING
● PLUS
RIDES RIDES RIDES
BUMPER BOATS SUPER SLIDE
X-AROUND ON THE MERRY GO ROUND,
AND MORE
● PLUS
LAZER LIGHT SHOW
● PLUS
ALCOHOL AVAILABLE ON PREMISES
RAVE DESIGN: THE WORLD FAMOUS THUNDER JOCKEYS
LIGHTING DESIGN: SCOTTO
$12 P.P. WITH INVITE $15 WITHOUT
TICKETS AVAILABLE AT TICKET MASTER CALL (212) 307-7171 AND HAPPENING STORES
SPONSORS
FLYING
INVASION RECORDINGS
GO BANG RECORDS
LIMELIGHT
BRAND X
R & S RECORDS

STORM
sr
NEW LOCATION
JULY 18, 1992
12:00 MIDNIGHT–9AM • 100% HARDCORE

Storm-rave must thank you, the ravers, for making June 20 a breath-taking experience. Now, we invite you to take the next step in rave culture. Our next show will take you further into the realms of hardcore raving. We will be featuring two female DJ's, plus we will continue to break the best upcoming rave-bands . . . Come and Join the Future.

Organization:
JOEY FAX
DAVE LIGHTS
MR. HYDE

Musical Coordination by:
FRANKIE BONES
Brooklyn Groove Prod.

TICKETS $15.00

Promotion Team
HEATHER HEATHER
FRED STRONG
NEIL RUSH

Rave Coordination by:
DENNIS THE MENACE
For Joint Ventures

STORM

PRESENTS
YOUR DESTINY
NEW YORK'S ORIGINATORS OF RAVE RETURNS: JULY 18, 1992
LIVE PERFORMANCES BY:

R&S RECORDS, BELGIUM
MUNDO MUSIQUE
"ACID PANDOMONIUM"
PLUS SECOND PHASE'S
"MENTASM"

ATMOSPHERE RECORDS, N.Y.
MASS HYSTERIA
FEATURING *SACRAFICE*
A LIVE TECHNO
DRAMA PERFORMANCE

DIRECT DRIVE RECORDS, NY
DISINTIGRATOR
"HUMAN"
& NEW TRACKS
OFF THEIR UPCOMING E.P.

B.G.P. RECORDS, N.Y.
X-CRASH
ADAM X & JIMMY CRASH
PLAYING UPCOMING CUTS
"STRESS" AND MORE

TECHNO-STORM DJ'S

FRANKIE BONES
PLAYING A LIVE SET ON 3 TURNTABLES
2 KEYBOARDS & 1 SAMPLER
4 YOUR N-JOY-MENT
A STORM EXCLUSIVE

FOR THE FIRST TIME EVER **STORM**
PRESENTS TWO OF THE BEST HARDCORE
FEMALE DJ'S IN AMERICA

JAQUELYN CHRISTIE from **DETROIT**
of "MAJESTIC" and "CITY" plus 96.3 FM

SANDRA COLLINS from **LOS ANGELES**
of PHOENIX'S UNDERGROUND and VARIOUS L.A. RAVES

— PLUS —

RALPHIE DEE
NEXT PLATEAU RECORDS

KEOKI
DISCO 2000

ADAM X
GROOVE

JIMMY CRASH
DIRECT DRIVE RECORDS

LENNY DEE
INDUSTRIAL
STRENGTH RECORDS

SHOW HOST : **FRANKIE BONES**
RAVE DANCIN' EXTRODINAIRE : **MISS MARCELINA**
COMPUTER ANIMATION BY : **ENO-ONE**

PLUS OTHERS TO BE CONFIRMED
40 K SOUND BY **FERARA & LOBOSO**

FOR INFO WRITE

2920 AVE. R
SUITE 137
BKLYN, NY 11229

TICKETS AVAILABLE FROM GROOVE RECORDS, 64 AVE U, BROOKLYN, NY FROM 8PM–2AM ON JULY 18
CALL (718) 714-5232 OR BEEP (718) 766-5369, SMART BAR, T-SHIRTS BOOTH, LASERS, NEW DANCE PLATFORMS,
DRINKS, GROOVE RECORD STAND, INTELLABEAMS, SYNCRO ENERGIZE MIND TOYS & MORE . . .

10 · 9 · 92
NASA

$12
TASTE OF THE FUTURE
MIND CANDY
Kool-Nasa
NRG-ENRICHED RAVE DRINK
WITH VITAMIN LOVE
LASTS ALL NIGHT   GOOD KARMA MIX SCOTTO+DB

NASA
MISSION CONTROL : DB + SCOTTO

NASA TIME CAPSULE ONE
LATE NIGHT SPACE SHUTTLE ARRAVAL
KEOKI
PLUS PLATINUM PLATTER PILOTS
DB • MR KLEEN
SOUL SLINGER

LIQUID SKY CAPSULE
PRESENTS
DJ ONE
DADDY LONG-LEGS + PAPA JOE

PSYCHECYBERADIANT LIGHTS : SCOTTO
DESIGN : CREATION UK + IQ
ALICE'S SMART BAR • MARTIN'S DUMB BAR
A PORTION OF PROCEEDS GO TO GREENPEACE

LIFTOFF : FRIDAY • 10 • 2 • 92 SPLASHDOWN : DAZEBREAK
FLIGHT : $10 W/FLYER BEFORE MIDNIGHT $12 AFTER

LAUNCH PAD : THE SHELTER
157 HUDSON ST
THREE BLOCKS BELOW CANAL

INFO : 212•330•8233 301•783•5492

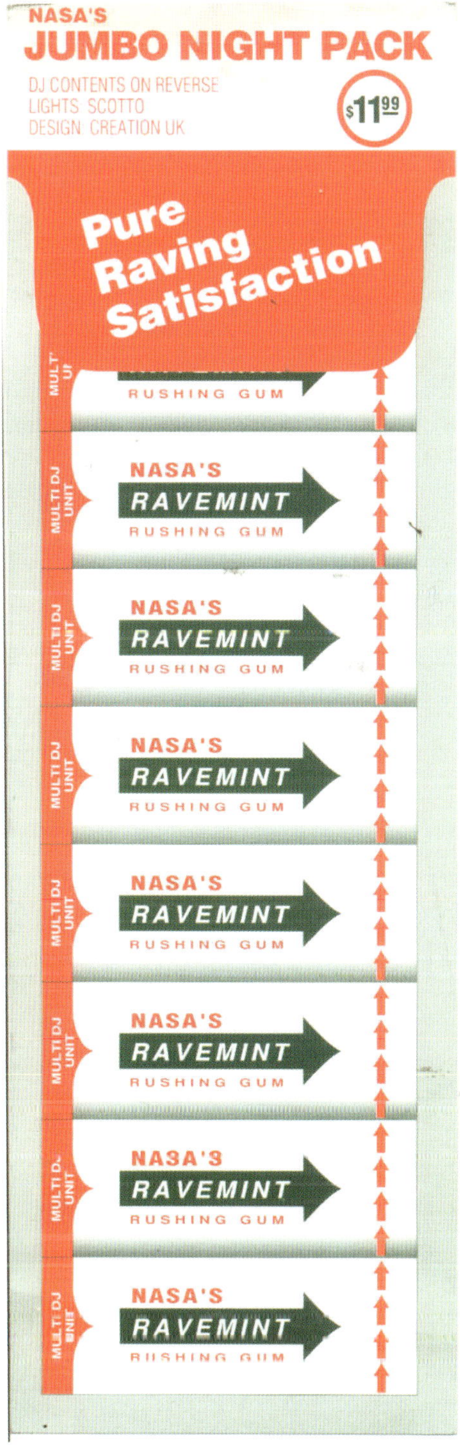

NASA'S
JUMBO NIGHT PACK
DJ CONTENTS ON REVERSE
LIGHTS: SCOTTO
DESIGN: CREATION UK
$11.99
Pure Raving Satisfaction
MULTI DJ UNIT
NASA'S RAVEMINT
RUSHING GUM
MULTI DJ UNIT
NASA'S RAVEMINT
RUSHING GUM
MULTI DJ UNIT
NASA'S RAVEMINT
RUSHING GUM
MULTI DJ UNIT
NASA'S RAVEMINT
RUSHING GUM
MULTI DJ UNIT
NASA'S RAVEMINT
RUSHING GUM
MULTI DJ UNIT
NASA'S RAVEMINT
RUSHING GUM
MULTI DJ UNIT
NASA'S RAVEMINT
RUSHING GUM
MULTI DJ UNIT
NASA'S RAVEMINT
RUSHING GUM

MISSION CONTROL: SCOTTO + DB

ASTRO DJ'S

DB + DANTE + ON-E + SOUL SLINGER

AUDIO VIBRATIONS

RAVE + TEKNO + BASTARD FAST HOUSE

LIQUID SKY ROOM

MR KLEEN + JASON JINX

AUDIO VIBRATIONS II

AMBIENT

STIMULANTS

SMART BAR + DUMB BAR

PSYCHCYBERADIANT LIGHTS

SCOTTO

VISUALS

XELIBRIUM + CREATION UK

HUMAN ACCEPTANCE

ALL AGES

STAR DATE

FRIDAY 9.4.92 • 11PM UNTIL DAZEBREAK

OUTPUT

$10 WITH INVITE TIL MIDNITE • $12 AFTER

LAUNCH PAD: THE SHELTER

157 HUDSON ST. 3 BLKS BELOW CANAL

RE-ENERGIZE 7:00AM

BREAKFAST + NASA DJ'S AT NEW LOCATION

RAVE LINE

212 330 8233 / BAL + DC 301 783 5492

DESIGN: CREATION UK + REB

NASA
FEDERATION
NOCTURNAL AUDIO
SENSORY AWAKENING
DB + SCOTTO
DEDICATED TO
PROTECT AND RAVE

NASA ORBITING DJ'S
DB + JASON JINX +ON-E + GUEST: MOBY

AUDIO VIBRATIONS
RAVE + TEKNO + BASTARD FAST HOUSE

LIQUID SKY ROOM DJ'S
MR KLEEN + TROPOSPHERE

AUDIO VIBRATIONS II
AMBIENT + TRANCE

STIMULANTS
SMART BAR + DUMB BAR

PSYCHCYBERADIANT LIGHTS
SCOTTO

HUMAN ACCEPTANCE
ALL AGES

STAR DATE
FRIDAY 11.13.92 • 11PM UNTIL DAZEBREAK

OUTPUT
$10 WITH INVITE TIL MIDNITE • $12 AFTER

LAUNCH PAD:THE SHELTER
157 HUDSON ST. 3 BLKS BELOW CANAL

RAVE LINE
1 800 RAVE LINE / 212 330 8233
BAL + DC 301 783 5492

DESIGN: CREATION UK + RE8

NASA ORBITING DJ'S
DB + JASON JINX + ON-E + GUEST: MOBY

AUDIO VIBRATIONS
RAVE + TEKNO + BASTARD FAST HOUSE

LIQUID SKY ROOM DJ'S
MR KLEEN + TROPOSPHERE

AUDIO VIBRATIONS II
AMBIENT + TRANCE

STIMULANTS
SMART BAR + DUMB BAR

PSYCHCYBERADIANT LIGHTS
SCOTTO

HUMAN ACCEPTANCE
ALL AGES

STAR DATE
FRIDAY 11.13.92 • 11PM UNTIL DAZEBREAK

OUTPUT
$10 WITH INVITE TIL MIDNITE • $12 AFTER

LAUNCH PAD:THE SHELTER
157 HUDSON ST. 3 BLKS BELOW CANAL

RAVE LINE
1 800 RAVE LINE / 212 330 8233
BAL + DC 301 783 5492

ORIGINAL
DOPE
FLAVOR
Nasooka
RUSHING GUM
MULTI
UNIT
DJ

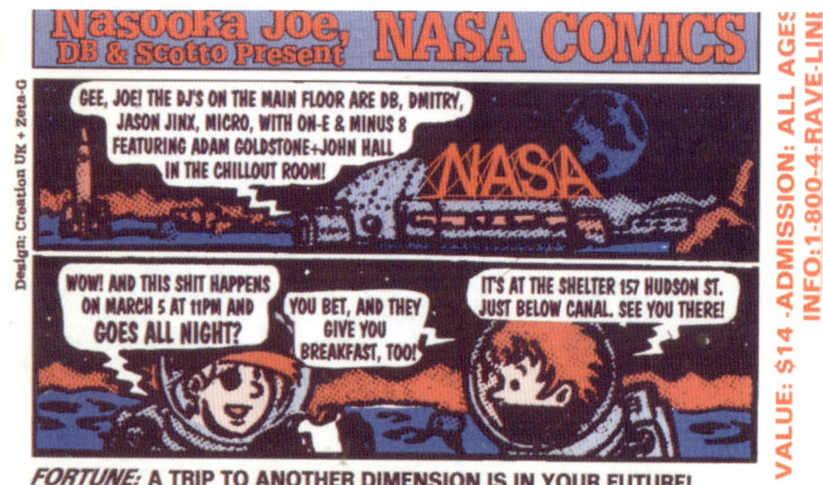

Nasooka Joe,
DB & Scotto Present
NASA COMICS
Design: Creation UK + Zeta-G
GEE, JOE! THE DJ'S ON THE MAIN FLOOR ARE DB, DMITRY, JASON JINX, MICRO, WITH ON-E & MINUS 8 FEATURING ADAM GOLDSTONE+JOHN HALL IN THE CHILLOUT ROOM!
NASA
WOW! AND THIS SHIT HAPPENS ON MARCH 5 AT 11PM AND GOES ALL NIGHT?
YOU BET, AND THEY GIVE YOU BREAKFAST, TOO!
IT'S AT THE SHELTER 157 HUDSON ST. JUST BELOW CANAL. SEE YOU THERE!
FORTUNE: A TRIP TO ANOTHER DIMENSION IS IN YOUR FUTURE!
VALUE: $14 -ADMISSION: ALL AGES
INFO:1-800-4-RAVE-LINE

NASA
AIR
+
SPACE

Caffeine

Tropi·nasa
PREMIUM RAVE
CONCENTRATED DJ FORCE

100% Pure
Florida Special
NASA JUICE
SUNSHINE POWERED
NET. NYC'S FINEST QUALITY PRODUCTION (1 PINT)

Florida Special
(divine aftermath)

Orbiting DJ Ingredients:
Sven Väth.... *(Germany)*
Dmitry......... *(Deee-lite)*
Keoki....... *(Disco 2000)*
DB.................. *(NASA)*

...plus suprise guests!!!

Psychecyberadiant Lights: Scotto

2 Sound Systems - 2 Rooms
Refuel at the Smart Bar

Launch Pad: 804 1st. St. (Bet. Alton Rd. & Washington Ave.)
Sunday, March 21, 1993: 10:00pm 'til YOU want to stop!

Human Acceptance: $7 with this flyer.
Underground Products Available

This is a NASA Production in association with Vinyl Trance Productions + SAD-D Productions

For Info, call (305) 532-3837

Design: Creation UK + Zeta-G

Caffeine

NASA PUBLICATION
UFO
WEEKLY
FRIDAY 28 MAY 1993 11PM $14
SPECIAL
EXTENDED NIGHT
EDITION
MORE HOURS FOR YOUR MONEY
CLOSE ENCOUNTERS OF THE DJ KIND
GUARANTEED PROVEN SIGHTINGS
WINK
DB
DESTRUCTO
JASON JINX
ON-E
RYDE
ODI
DAVE THE WAVE
DORIAN
MORNING GLORY MIX
DANTE
nasa
'NASA CHILDREN'
SCIENCE CAN'T EXPLAIN THEIR EXISTANCE!
-WHERE DO THEY COME FROM?
-WHAT DO THEY WANT?
INSIDE: EXCLUSIVE ANSWERS
NASA: MISSION CONTROL-THE SHELTER. 157 HUDSON ST. NYC. $9 BEFORE 12 WITH INVITE. $14 AFTER.
UFO WEEKLY: FOR SUBSCRIPTIONS AND SIGHTINGS, CALL 212-330-8233.
EXTRATERRESTRIAL LIGHTS: SCOTTO + JOSH. GRAPHIX: DB FOR CREATION UK + ZETA-G.

Natural High 2
August 19, 1994

FRIDAY, AUGUST 19, 1994 STARTING TIME 10PM
UNTILL 12 NOON SATURDAY
Natural High 2
At
Caffeine
DEGO
reinforced
DJ ICEE
orlando
WINK
sorted, philly
DAVE TRANCE
caffiene
SCOTT RICHMOND
net-upnorth
FRANKIE BONES
groove
FEELGOOD
fever, baltimore
DEBO
mindwarp boston
DNA
caffiene
MICRO
caffiene
NIGEL RICHARDS
611 records uk
SAMEER
caffiene
$10 W/FLYER
$12 W/OUT
NO GUEST LIST
18 AND OVER
PROPER ID
REQUIRED
THIS IS THE 2ND IN A SERIES OF
4 ALL NIGHT PARTIES
LOCATION: CAFFEINE 836 GRAND BLVD - DIX HILLS NY
DIRECTIONS
LIE EXPRWY: EXIT 52 SOUTH (COMMACK RD) 3MILES TO
GRAND BLVD (7-11 ON CORNER) MAKE LEFT-1/2 MILE ON RIGHT
SOUTHERN STATE: EXIT 39 NORTH (RT231) TO COMMACK RD
1 MILE GRAND BLVD (7-11 ON CORNER)MAKE RIGHT-1/2 MILE ON RIGHT
BY TRAIN: TAKE L.I.R.R. TO DEER PARK STATION
CALL 516 822 LIRR FOR TRAIN TIMES
FREE SHUTTLE FROM DEER PARK STATION TO CAFFEINE
LONG ISLAND
caffiene 516.242.1773
kort&gregg 516.547.7118
rabbit 516.724.1136
toast 516.345.5517
MANHATTEN
scooter 212.479.7760
alan sanctuary 212.696.8938
PHILLY
611 Rec 215.413.9100
BALTIMORE
ultraworld 410.880.7031
BOSTON
primary 617.499.7765
BROOKLYN
twr 718.390.8923
PROMO THANKS:
kort,gregg,rabbit,toast,primary,
harv-e,robin,allie,stoffer,tim,will,611,
alan sanctuary,twr,donya,scooter,
jeff h,upnorth,ultraworld,fever
and all thoes who support us
COMING SEPTEMBER 1ST AND 2ND
CAFFEINES FIRST 48HR SUMMER PARTY

Natural High

NATURAL HIGH
at Caffeine

DJs
DOC MARTIN
LAWRENCE
OF GAT DECOR
JAMES CHRISTIAN
SAMEER
SPACE ACE
MICRO

DJs
KEOKI
GUY DMC
DAVE TRANCE
TROPOSPERE
BOBBLE
RYDE
ONIONZ

friday june 11th 1993
10pm till 12 noon sat
THIS IS THE 1st IN A SERIES OF 4 ALL NIGHT PARTIES
NO GUEST LIST !

PROMOS
KORT & GREG • TREPP • EDDIE VAN RAVEN •
TOAST & BRAD • JEFF HANSON • SLIPSHOD ROB •
STEVEN.A • MELLO MELLO (NYC) • CHRIS STYLES (BALT)
SCOOTER(NJ) • MARC (DEL) • SAM I AM (DC) • DIRT (BOST)

$10 W/FLYER
$12 W/OUT

18 AND OVER
PROPER ID
REQUIRED
A&A Graphics
718.821.8784

LOCATION: Caffeine 836 Grand Blvd • Dix Hills NY
DIRECTIONS:
LIE EXPRWY: Exit 52 South (Commack Road) 3 miles to
Grand Blvd (corner 7/11) Make Left 1/2 mile on right
SOUTHERN STATE: Exit 39 north (RT 231) to Commack
Road 1 mile Grand Blvd (corner 7-11) make right 1/2 mile on RT
BY TRAIN: Take L.I.R.R. to Deer Park Station • trains leave
N.Y. Penn Station at 10:14 • 11:14 • 12:15 • 1:14 • 2:46 • 5:14
There will be a free shuttle bus from Deer Park Station to Caffeine

Long Island • 516.242.1773
• 516.547.7118
• 516.547.6129
N.Y.C. • 212.629.1960
• 212.683.1358
New Jersey • 201.927.2292
Delaware • 302.453.8567
D.C. • 202.638.2728
Boston • 617.730.9476
• 617.499.4848
Baltimore • 410.752.7305

Caffeine
Eternal Summer

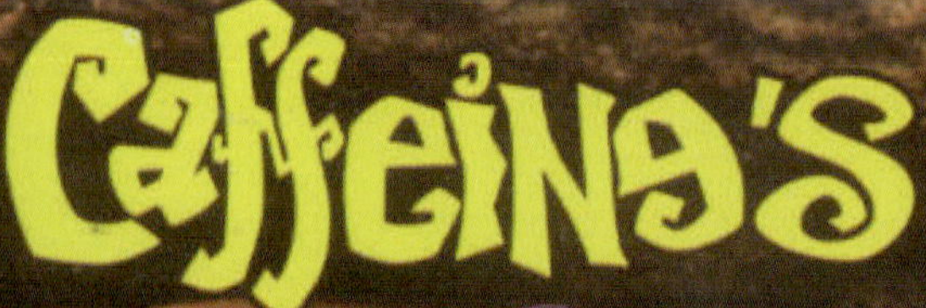

Caffeine's

Eternal Summer
A New Beginning...
FRIDAY, MAY 27th, 1994
the Season's First All Night Party
Leading Us into the Light:

NIGEL RICHARDS
(611 Records, Philly)
DNA • SAMEER
DAVE TRANCE
PETE PANIC (LI)

MICRO
WHO (B'more)
SUN (Ultraworld)
SEIGE (LI)
TERRA (B'klyn)

On the Outdoor Deck

Ambient Acoustics by
DJ ENTITY (ultraworld)

Synchro-Energize   Body Piercing by
with STOUFER   BODY DESIGNS
$2 OFF WITH INVITE
18 and Over • Proper ID Required
Promotions: That's Krafty and the Caffeine Crew

836 Grand Blvd., Dix Hills, NY 11729 • 516.242.1773
LIE East Exit 52 Commack Rd. South to Grand Blvd., (corner 7/11) make left, club is 1/2 mile on right. LIE
West Exit 53 Service Rd. to Commack Rd., make left, follow above directions.
SS Pkwy. Exit 39N Rte 231 - fork right on Commack Rd. to Grand Blvd. (Corner 7/11) make right, club is
1/2 mile on right.
Safe, Secure Parking Available at Deer Park LIRR Station Free Shuttlebus to and from Caffeine all night long.

natural high 4

natural high 4

@ Caffeine

this is the 4th in a series of all night parties

10:00PM FRIDAY NOV 19 TILL 10:00AM SATURDAY

djs

micro caffeine	**sameer** caffeine	**scott henry** baltimore
jason jinx long island		**armand** strictly rhythm records
reade novamute records	**guy dmc** dmc records	**troposphere** dmc records
bob bentley england	**denard** nyc	**osheen** rhode island
nigel philly	**dna** caffeine	**dave trance** caffeine

24 HOUR INFO LINES

LONG ISLAND

516-242-1773

516-547-6129

516-547-7118

516-724-1136

NYC

212-631-4290

212-696-8938

212-631-1033

PROMOTIONS:

Kort & Greg, Mello, Trepp
Eddie Van Raven, Scooter
Alan Sanctuary, Energizer Rabbit
Jeff H., Slipshod Rob, Chris Stiles
Toast, Rad Brad, Sam I Am
Dustin (Boston), E-Force (NJ)

$10 W/PASS • $12 W/OUT
NO GUEST LIST • 18 & OVER • PROPER ID REQUIRED

L.I.E.: Exit 52S (Commack Rd) at Grand Blvd (corner 7-11) make left 1/2 mile on right.
SOUTHERN STATE: Exit 39N (Rt. 231) to Commack Rd 1 mile make right onto Grand Blvd (corner 7-11).
PENN STATION: Ron Kon Koma branch to Deer Park, leaving at 10:14, 11:14, 12:15, 1:14, 2:46, 5:14, Free Shuttle to Caffeine.

Get ▶ NEW YEAR'S EVE PT II
Set ▶ 48 HR MARATHON

design: Zetagy

Caffeine

Friday August 4th, 1995

Micro   DNA

James Christian

X-Dream   Dave Trance

Giveaways all night • Open Bar till 11:30

Polygram & Point Music give you
Music for the Millenium featuring:
**Todd Levin   Gavin Bryars
(Aphex Twin) Remixes and Glenn Branca**

Admission: $8 with pass 18& over/$6 with pass 21& over
Adv Tix @ Bugg (516) 797-7196
Info: (516) 242-1773   (516) 951-1170

Directions: **LIE EAST:** EXIT 52 MAKE RIGHT ONTO COMMACK RD, GO 3 MILES TO GRAND BLVD. CORNER OF 7-11. MAKE LEFT AT LIGHT. CLUB IS HALF MILE ON RIGHT.
LIE WEST: EXIT 53. FOLLOW SERVICE ROAD TO COMMACK RD. (COUNTY ROAD 4) MAKE LEFT. FOLLOW DIRECTIONS ABOVE.
SOUTHERN STATE: EXIT 39 NORTH. GO HALF MILE. FORK RIGHT ONTO COMMACK ROAD. GO 2 MILES TO GRAND BLVD. (CORNER 7-11). MAKE RIGHT AT LIGHT. CLUB IS HALF MILE ON RIGHT.

UNITED NATIONS
OF NASA.

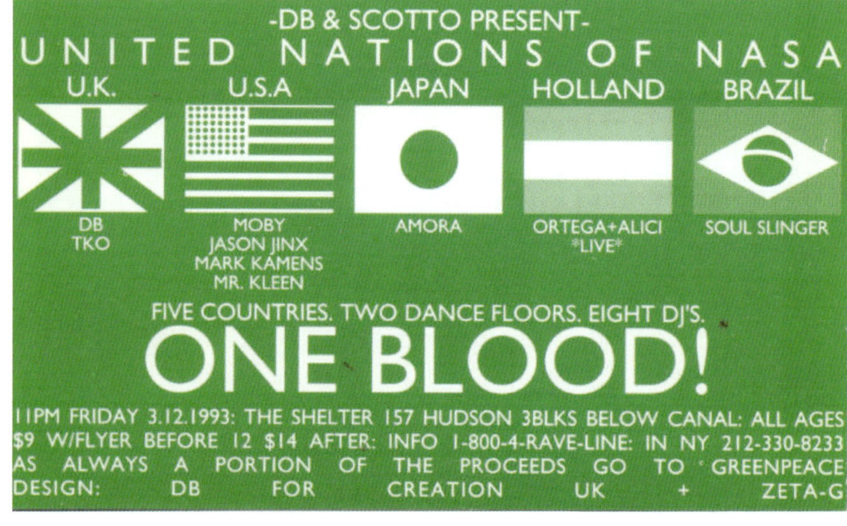

-DB & SCOTTO PRESENT-
UNITED NATIONS OF NASA
U.K.   U.S.A   JAPAN   HOLLAND   BRAZIL
DB   MOBY   AMORA   ORTEGA+ALICI   SOUL SLINGER
TKO   JASON JINX   *LIVE*
         MARK KAMENS
         MR. KLEEN
FIVE COUNTRIES. TWO DANCE FLOORS. EIGHT DJ'S.
ONE BLOOD!
11PM FRIDAY 3.12.1993: THE SHELTER 157 HUDSON 3BLKS BELOW CANAL: ALL AGES
$9 W/FLYER BEFORE 12 $14 AFTER: INFO 1-800-4-RAVE-LINE: IN NY 212-330-8233
AS ALWAYS A PORTION OF THE PROCEEDS GO TO GREENPEACE
DESIGN: DB   FOR   CREATION   UK   +   ZETA-G

nasa
present
BOOM!

present

Solar Flaring
Live Performances:

808 STATE

meat Beat MANIFESTO

supreme love gods

Goin' Global™ DJs:

Moby	*NYC*
DB	*NASA*
Keoki	*Disco 2000*
Wink	*Philly*
Destructo	*Rave America*
Micro	*L.I.*
On-E	*NASA*
Tony Fletcher	*Communion*
Mr. Kleen	*NASA*
Sean CIC	*Anarchic*

plus after hours with:

Dmitry	*Deee-lite*
Soul Slinger	*Liquid Sky*
Joeski	*NASA*

spinning in two rooms
on hyper-powered
surround sound systems

Lighting up the Heavens:
Psychecyberadiant™ Scotto

Visual Astrophysics:
808's Incredible Lasers

Experience Manhattan's biggest, boldest, baddest,
bustproof all night dance frenzy! at the world famous

ROSELAND BALLROOM

239 West 52nd St. (at Broadway)
Tickets $15 in advance at Bleeker Bobs or $17 at door.

Star Date™: Saturday, April 17, 1993.
11pm 'till 6am. INFO: 212-330-8233.

PRODUCED BY DB AND SCOTTO IN DEEP SPACE

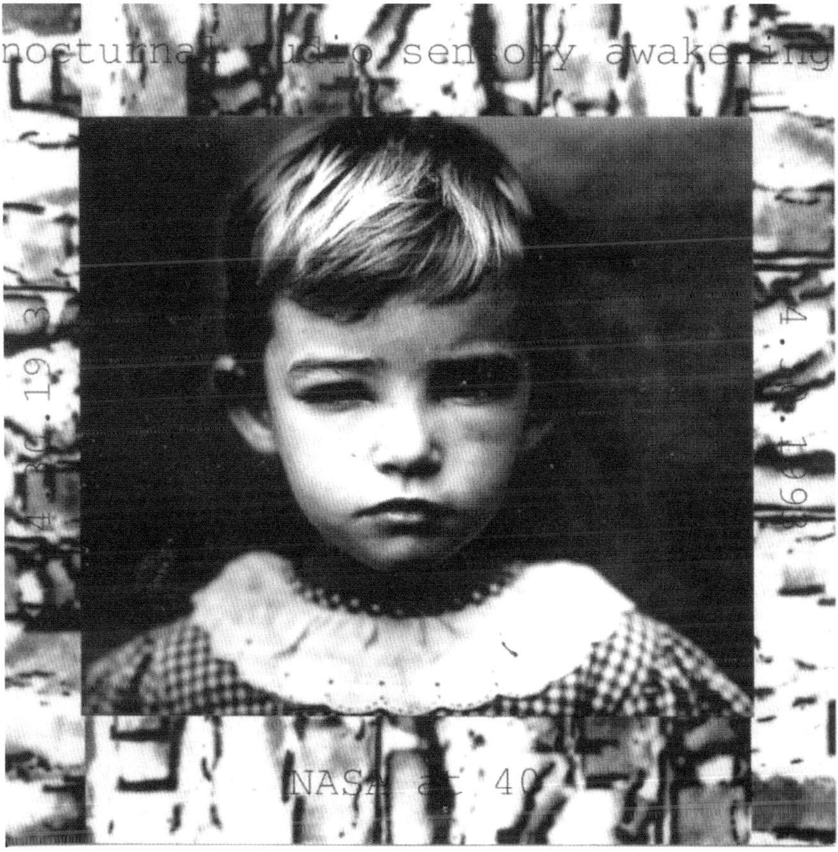

nocturnal audio sensory awakening
NASA at 40

R A V E R ' S
LIFE
nasa
Babies are SMARTER than you Think

Children
Genetically
Engineered to DJ
before they could speak.
DB
Jason Jinx
On-E
Denard
K-Tel + Chester.
Special guest
DJ Heart.

nasa

July 2, 1993
50th NASA!!!

07

0 724444 9

Psychecyberadiant Lights: Scotto.
11pm. $9 with flyer before 12. $14 after. Ages 16 and up. At the Shelter, 157 Hudson St. NYC.
NASA infoline: (212) 330-8233. Graphics: DB for Creation UK and Zeta-G for Drop Entertainment.